The Magic Circus

Wayne Anderson

story told by
Christopher Logue

A Studio Book
The Viking Press · New York

For Nick, Rosy and Lizzie

Also by Wayne Anderson and Christopher Logue
RATSMAGIC

Text Copyright © Jonathan Cape Limited, 1979
Illustrations Copyright © Wayne Anderson, 1979
Published in 1979 by The Viking Press
625 Madison Avenue, New York, N.Y. 10022

Library of Congress Catalog Card Number: 78-24761
ISBN 0-670-44809-5
Printed in Great Britain

Early on midsummer's day the Magic Circus gathered beside
the foot-path that led through the forest to Hippodrome Place.

King Twig read out the *List of Performers* and Queen Crinkle
checked to see that everyone was in the procession.

"Captain Humperson, The Strong Man," King Twig called.
"Present!" said Captain Humperson.
"The Band," said King Twig.
"Here!" said Mr Fiddler, Percy the Bassoonist, and Banjo Dan.
"Lion," said King Twig.
And the Lion gave a growl.
"Big Beryl, The Fat Lady, and Mr One-By-Ten, The Tallest Clown
in the World," said King Twig.
"Present," said Big Beryl.
"Present," said Mr One-By-Ten.

When he had worked through the list King Twig said:
"Bandsmen, strike up the *Tightrope March*!"

And following the sound of the music the Circus began their
walk to Hippodrome Place where, when the sun had set, they
would give their Great Annual Show.

"Pardon my asking," said Banjo Dan as he marched along, "but
is it always so dark at this time of day?"
Banjo Dan was new to the Circus. The forest made him uneasy.

"Stop talking and march straight ahead," said Captain Humperson.

All the same, Banjo Dan was right; it was getting dark.
In the end it became pitch black. You could not see a hand
in front of your face.

"Circus, about turn!" said King Twig.

When they turned about they saw the way back was barred by huge white thorns, and they heard a titter that changed into a scratchy voice, saying:

"Hee-hee-hee-hee … My name is Growser. Doctor Growser, The World's Cleverest Conjuror. And I hate all circuses!"

"Not the *Magic* Circus?" said Mr One-By-Ten.

"*All* circuses," said Doctor Growser. "None of them will let a conjuror as clever as myself become World Famous. So I hate them *all* – including yours."

Everybody held hands in the darkness. Even Captain Humperson was afraid.

"Do you think you could tell us where we are?" Queen Crinkle asked.

"With the greatest of pleasure," said Doctor Growser. "You have walked into the mouth of my monster, Megalump. The huge white thorns you can see are Megalump's teeth. And if I say 'Megalump, swallow!' none of you will ever be seen again."

"However," Doctor Growser continued, "for the moment I shall not order Megalump to swallow. Instead, one by one you will come out of his mouth and show me your acts. If anyone has a trick I have not seen before – well, I may let him (or her) go. Now, which one of you will be the first to perform?"

"I will," said King Twig.

But Queen Crinkle would not hear of it.

"Send the Lion," she said. "The Lion will make a meal of him."

"I am not feeling hungry," said the Lion.

"He is bound to know all my tricks," said the One Wheel Mouse.

"And mine," said Mr One-By-Ten.

"Hurry up!" said Doctor Growser.

"Let me go," said Miss Mint of The Flying Mints, Aerial Artists Extraordinary.

"And I will follow my friend Mint," said Big Beryl.

"Open, Megalump!" said Doctor Growser.

So Megalump opened and allowed Mint to step out on to his lower lip.

"Begin," said Doctor Growser.

Mint waited until a bee flew under Megalump's nose. Then, spreading her wings, she tiptoed on to the bee's velvet shoulders and swooped about the air.

"Bravo!" shouted the Circus as they looked between Megalump's teeth.

"Seen it! Seen it!" said Doctor Growser and cracked his knuckles so loudly the bee lurched sideways in the air and toppled Mint on to the ground.

"Boo! . . ." cried the Circus.

"Next!" said Doctor Growser.

"That means me," said Big Beryl.

It was then Banjo Dan had his idea for their escape.

"Captain Humperson," he whispered, "can you lift Big Beryl?"
"I can lift anything," said the Captain.
"Then get Beryl on to your shoulders," said Banjo Dan, "and when you are standing on Megalump's lip – *jump.*"

Lifting Big Beryl was not easy.
Her dress size was 1000·5.
The Lion often slept
in one of her shoes.
But Captain Humperson
managed it.

"Keep close to Beryl
and the Captain," Banjo Dan told the rest of the Circus.

Grunting and groaning the Captain staggered past Megalump's teeth and on to his lip.

"Coo-eee! . . ." said Big Beryl to Doctor Growser.
Doctor Growser frowned.
"Jump!" said Banjo Dan.
"Wait!" yelled Doctor Growser.
But the Doctor was a moment too slow.

Captain Humperson jumped and Whooooosh! through the air he and Big Beryl went, landing with a gigantic belly-flop that emptied a forest pool by Megalump's feet.

"Swallow, Megalump! Swallow!" shouted Doctor Growser.

But Megalump did not obey his master.

The sight of Big Beryl's belly-flop made him roar with laughter. And the longer and louder Megalump laughed, the wider and wider he opened his jaws.

"Follow me!" shouted Banjo Dan.

And quick as a flash the Circus dropped from Megalump's mouth on to the floor of the forest and dashed away into the undergrowth.

"Run for the Giant Bluebells," said King Twig.

"I'll get you! I'll get you!" shrieked Doctor Growser.

"On the contrary," said Captain Humperson, "I'll get *you!*"

And he grabbed the Doctor by the scruff of his neck, flung him over his shoulder, and followed King Twig.

Handing Doctor Growser over to the Lion, Captain Humperson grabbed the tallest of the bluebells and bent its stem towards the ground.

"Everyone climb on to my hands!" he shouted. And up they all climbed – Queen Crinkle holding Doctor Growser firmly by the ear.

Then Captain Humperson said:

"Ready?"

"Ready!" the Circus replied.

"Steady?"

"Steady!" the Circus replied. And as the word "go" sprang to Captain Humperson's lips he caught Mr One-By-Ten by the ankle, released the Giant Bluebell's stem, and:

"GO!"

everybody shouted together as the bluebell whipped back to its proper height and catapulted the Circus and Doctor Growser far into the sky.

Up, and up, and up, and up they went until Megalump was no more than a dot on a green cloth far below them.

"What happens when we land?" said Banjo Dan.

"We will all be killed!" moaned Doctor Growser.

"Not if I know Captain Humperson," said King Twig.

"Prepare for landing," cried Captain Humperson.

Using his great strength the Captain swung them all head-over-heels in mid air until his feet were pointing towards the ground.

"As we hit the floor – everybody relax and shout *Bingo*!" he cried.

One second before landing Captain Humperson braced his thighs until the muscles bulged like sails. Then with a shout of:

"BINGO!"
the Circus landed.

I will not say it was a *perfect* touch-down; more of a
"bounce-down"; but apart from a few bruises no
one was hurt.

Doctor Growser came off the worst. He was thrown into
the middle of an outsize spider's web. The sticky threads
twined round him and he could not move an inch.

"I wonder where we are," said Big Beryl as she rubbed
her behind.
"Poor Beryl," said Mint, "I will go and find you some
dock leaves to rub on it."

"What about *me*?" said Doctor Growser. "I am stuck in
this loathsome web."
"And there you will stay until we have decided what
to do with you," said Queen Crinkle.

"Come here, everyone! Come and see what I have found!"
called Mint.

Mr One-By-Ten was the first to reach her side.
"Look," she said and pointed through the trees. "It's
Hippodrome Place!"

And so it was. A hundred yards from where they had landed
they could see the turf of their annual performing ground.

"It looks as if we can give our performance after all,"
said King Twig.

No sooner had the Circus and the Doctor vanished into the blue than Megalump stopped laughing and realised that he was alone.

And if there was one thing Megalump hated it was being alone.

When Megalump gave a mighty sniff, all he could smell was the forest. When Megalump bellowed, only the echo of his bellow returned to his ears. And when Megalump looked up, or down, to the right, or to the left, he saw nothing but leaves.

"How shall I find Doctor Growser?" Megalump asked himself. "Look," Megalump answered himself.

Not, you will notice, "Where shall I look?" or even "In what direction shall I look?" but simply "Megalump, look!"; rather like "Megalump, swallow!" – only different.

Having got as far as "Look!", Megalump saw no reason to delay. Fixing his eyes straight before him and putting his best foot forward Megalump stomped off into the forest.

While King Twig and the rest of the Circus began to
get Hippodrome Place ready for the Great Show, Banjo Dan
and Captain Humperson went to see Doctor Growser in
the spider's web.

The Doctor's temper was much the same as before.
"Cut me free at once," he snapped.
"Surely the World's Cleverest Conjuror can escape from
a spider's web without help?" said Captain Humperson.
"As a matter of fact," said Doctor Growser, "I have often
escaped from trickier spots than this. But for the moment
I have forgotten how."

"Well," said Banjo Dan, "you have plenty of time to
remember how. The Great Show does not begin until midnight,
and I am sure you will have escaped long before it gets dark."

"Dark?" squeaked the Doctor. "You would leave me trapped
in this web after dark?"
"We might leave you there forever – unless you change your
mind about our Magic Circus," said Captain Humperson.
"Magic-Smagic," said the Doctor in his rudest voice.

"Shall we see if Mr One-By-Ten has stretched the tightrope?"
Banjo Dan said to the Captain.
"Good idea," said the Captain.
"Don't leave me!" shouted Doctor Growser.

But Banjo Dan and Captain Humperson strolled away from him
without looking back.

After Megalump had stomped through the forest for more than an hour it began to dawn on him that he was no nearer to finding Doctor Growser and the Circus.

At this point most of us would sit down for a good long think.

But thinking was not Megalump's strongest point. Instead of sitting down, Megalump changed his stomp to a galumph. That is to say, he went through the forest twice as fast as before.

And as he galumphed along like a castle on stilts Megalump changed his bellow from Bellow Normal to Bellow Loud.

But hour 1 slipped into hour 2 and still he was alone. Then Bellow Loud became Bellow Deafening, but still nobody replied.

In the end Megalump became convinced that he would be alone for the rest of his life.
As he had changed his Stomp into a Galumph, so he changed his Galumph into a Galumphelton, and, as he roared along, Megalump tossed great clumps and groves of trees into the air and the forest floor trembled beneath his feet.

"This will be the end of the forest ..." said an Acorn to an Oak. "It will be the end of the world!" replied the Oak.

In Hippodrome Place the tightrope had
been stretched and One Wheel Mouse
was ready to practise his act.

"Mouse, are you prepared?"
said King Twig.
"I am," said Mouse.

And carrying his cycle on his
back Mouse nipped up the tree,
balanced his wheel on the tightrope, and pedalled out into
thin air ...

King Twig held his breath. After being swallowed (or almost
swallowed) and catapulted through space would Mouse keep
his balance?

Wobbling a little from side to side Mouse reached the
middle of the tightrope.
"Keep going, Mouse!" shouted Queen Crinkle.

But to everybody's surprise Mouse did nothing of the kind.

Pedalling first forwards and then backwards Mouse stood up
in the saddle and began to wave his arms about.
"It must be a new part of his act," said Big Beryl to Mint.

Then Mouse began to cry out: "Run for your lives! Run for
your lives! I can see Megalump rushing towards us!
Unless he can be stopped we will all be squashed flat!"

As if to prove his words the ground began to tremble
and they heard Bellow Deafening coming over the trees ...

"Get the Doctor," said King Twig.

Banjo Dan and Captain Humperson cut the threads of the spider's web and rushed the Doctor to Hippodrome Place.

"Hurry," cried Mouse. "Megalump is getting nearer!"

"Doctor," said King Twig, "you claim to be the World's Cleverest Conjuror?"

"I do," said Doctor Growser.
"Then now is your chance to prove it," said King Twig.
"If you can stop Megalump we will let you join the Magic Circus and make you World Famous."

Everyone waited to hear what Doctor Growser would say. Doctor Growser sulked and said nothing.

And the pounding of Megalump's feet began to shake the trees.

"Help!" cried Mouse as he slipped from the tightrope into Captain Humperson's arms.

"Doctor!" shouted King Twig, "we have only a few seconds left. Megalump will not care who he is crushing. You will be squashed, too!"

But still Doctor Growser did nothing.

"Please," said Mint. "I really believe in your skill."

"Very well," said Doctor Growser.
"I will stop Megalump."
"How?" said King Twig.
"With the Iron Bubble," said Doctor Growser.
"Where will we find an Iron Bubble?"
said Banjo Dan.
"In my top hat," said the Doctor.

Taking his top hat from his head,
Doctor Growser walked straight into
Megalump's path.

"Bubble – appear!" he commanded and felt about in his hat.
Out popped a rabbit.
"Bubble – appear!" he cried in a sterner voice.
Out popped a elephant ridden by a tiny soldier.
"*Bubble – appear!*" the Doctor repeated at the top of his voice.

But command as often as he might and feel about in his hat as
much as he could, out popped butterfly cards, moth cards,
a mermaid bearing a key, several kinds of birds, more cards,
everything except an Iron Bubble.

"We are done for!" Captain Humperson said.
And Megalump crashed through the trees into Hippodrome Place!
But the Doctor stood his ground.

"By my Father, my Grandfather,
and my Great Grandfather,
World Famous Conjurors All,
IRON BUBBLE – APPEAR!"
he cried.

And lo and behold an enormous
globe of transparent iron
grew out of the Doctor's top hat.

Even as Megalump's feet were about to stamp Doctor Growser
into the forest floor he was imprisoned in the bubble's
glowing wall!

The sound of Megalump's bellow died away, the ground
stopped trembling, and the sunlight filled Hippodrome
Place.

"Three cheers for Doctor Growser – The World's Greatest
Conjuror, the Star of the Magic Circus!" said King Twig.

"Hooray!" cheered the Circus. "Hooray! Hooray!"

"Hooray!" cried Megalump.
Bubble or no bubble Megalump was quite content now that
he was no longer alone.

"And now," said King Twig, "let us begin the Great Annual Show!"